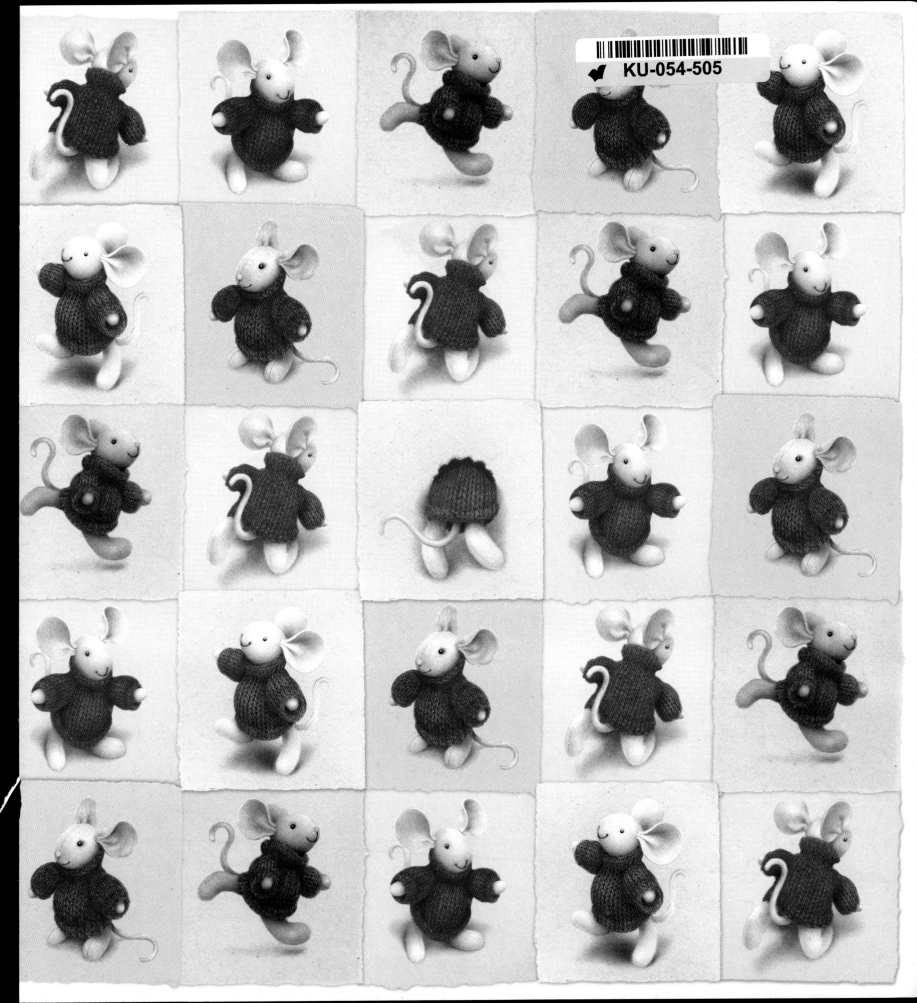

For Isabelle

SALARIYA

www.salariya.com

shop online

shop.salariya.com

This edition published in Great Britain in MMXIII
by Scribblers, a division of Book House, an imprint of
The Salariya Book Company Ltd
25 Marlborough Place,
Brighton BN1 1UB

www.scribblersbooks.com
www.janehissey.co.uk

© The Salariya Book Company Ltd MMXIII
Text and illustrations © Jane Hissey MMXIII

HB ISBN-13: 978-1-908973-43-6

PB ISBN-13: 978-1-908973-44-3

3 5 7 9 8 6 4 2

A CIP catalogue record for this book is
available from the British Library.

Printed and bound in China
Printed on paper from sustainable sources
Reprinted in MMXIII

Ruby, Blue and Blanket

Jane Hissey

Ruby, Blanket and Blue were planning a game.
'Let's play dressing up, so we don't look the same.
We'll wear different things and we'll be in disguise –
And let's give the funniest one a big prize.'

Blanket looked through a box for something to wear,
He thought about stripes or some long yellow hair.
'I could be a zebra, but better than that,
I'll dress up as a unicorn, wearing this hat!'

Blue Rabbit chose hair and a flowery dress,
'I just need a crown and I'll be a princess.
You can all bring me jewels and nice things to eat,
And I shall wear nothing at all on my feet.'

Now Ruby decided a witch would work well,
With a hat and a broomstick she made up a spell,
And in through the window flew billions of bats
And saucers of milk for some very small cats.

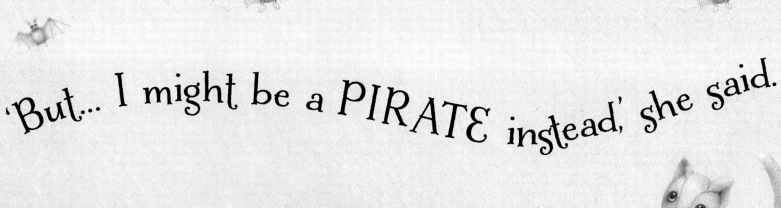

'But... I might be a PIRATE instead,' she said.

With an eyepatch and parrot (who squawked 'All Aboard!')
She walked up the gang-plank, waving her sword.
'I've sailed seven seas and I see land at last,'
She called from the top of the pirate ship's mast.

'Hmmm... I might be a FAIRY instead,' she said.

With her own magic wand and her butterfly wings
And some fairy dust that she sprinkled on things,
She painted the flowers that grew all around –
And she painted anything else that she found!

'Ah... I could be a COWBOY instead,' she said.

'I would ride very fast holding on to my hat
And lasso a cactus and sleep on a mat.
I would cook my baked beans and wash up in a lake.
I wouldn't be lonely: I'd have a pet snake.'

'Well... I could be a GHOST instead,' she said.

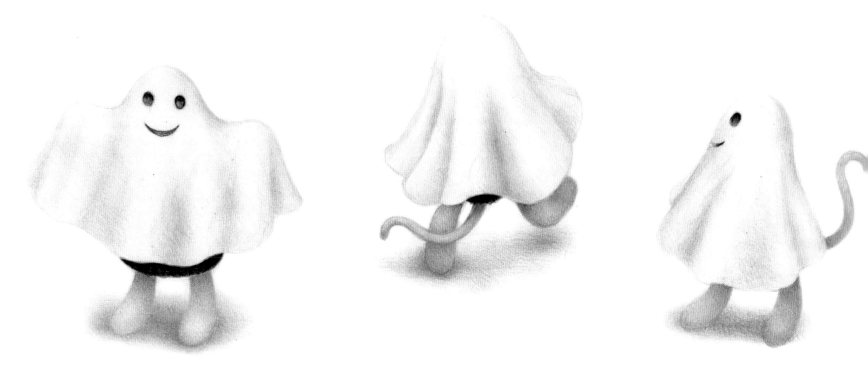

'I would be all shapeless and floaty and white,
And tiptoe around in my sheet in the night.
And if anyone said, 'Are ghosts really true?'
I'd jump out and surprise them by bellowing...

BOO!'

'Or... I could be a MERMAID instead,' she said.

Ruby liked her long hair and her fishtail feet.

She swam in the sea and had seaweed to eat.

But she sat on the rocks and she started to wish

There was someone to play with who wasn't a fish.

'So... I could be a SPACEMAN instead,' she said.

'I would fly in a rocket right up to the stars,
Have lunch on the moon and supper on Mars,
Play spaceball with little green alien men,
Then wave from my spaceship and fly home again.'

'Oh... I just can't DECIDE,' she cried.

Then Ruby sat down on the floor and she sighed,
'I really can't choose what to wear – and I've tried.
Is the cowboy hat best, or the fishtail feet?
Or the wings or the wand or the ghosty, white sheet?'

'I JUST CAN'T DECIDE!' she cried.

'Don't worry,' said Blanket, 'You don't have to choose.
We'll mix up the hats and the costumes and shoes.
Then we'll dress ourselves up in a mixture of things.
We'll be pirates in spaceships and cowboys with wings!'

So Blanket dressed up as a four-legged fairy
With a unicorn horn, while Ruby went hairy.

Blue Rabbit, the mer-witch, waved from his broom
As he scattered seashells around in the room.

And Ruby jumped up in the air and she cried,
'This is such fun; I don't have to decide.
I can wear anything! I can be what I wish –
A pirate princess or a unicorn fish!'

'And the prize will be shared!' she declared.

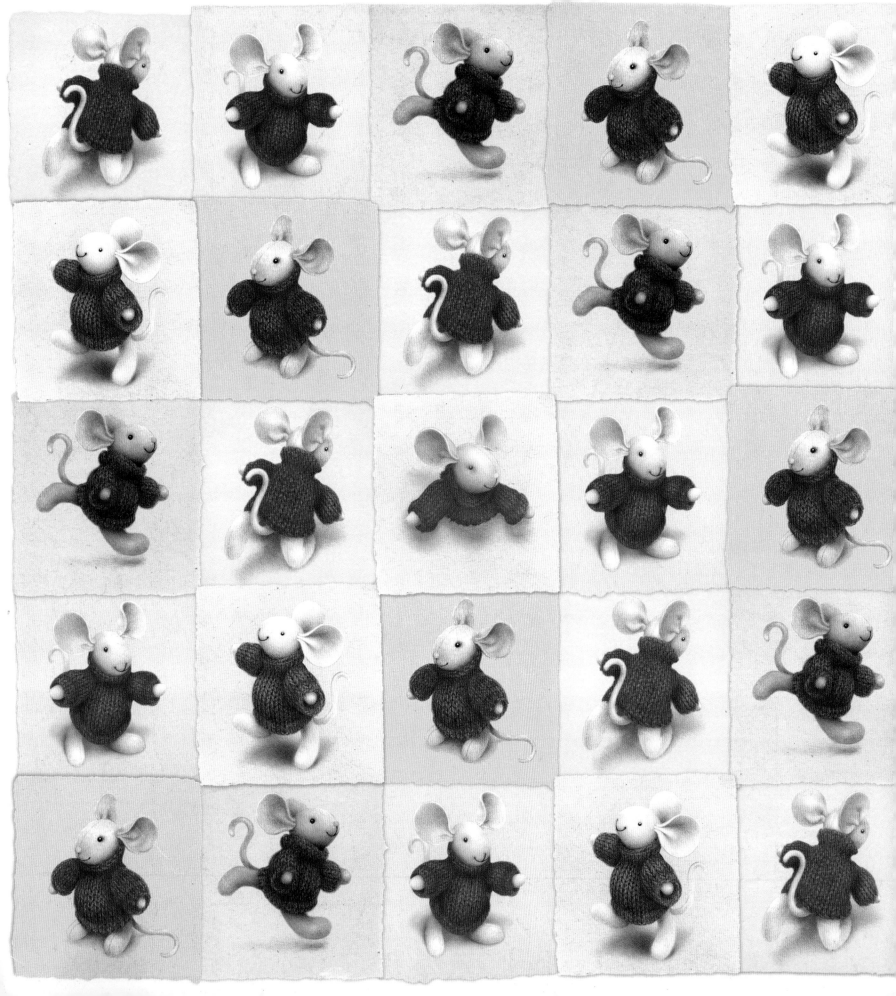